LITTLE GOLDEN BOOK® CLASSICS
Featuring the art of
Tibor Gergely

Three Best-Loved Tales

TOOTLE
By Gertrude Crampton

THE HAPPY MAN AND HIS DUMP TRUCK
By Miryam

SCUFFY THE TUGBOAT
By Gertrude Crampton

A GOLDEN BOOK • NEW YORK
Western Publishing Company, Inc., Racine, Wisconsin 53404

TOOTLE

By Gertrude Crampton

Far, far to the west of everywhere is the village of Lower Trainswitch. All the baby locomotives go there to learn to be big locomotives. The young locomotives steam up and down the tracks, trying to call out the long, sad "ToooOooot" of the big locomotives. But the best they can do is a gay little "Tootle."

Lower Trainswitch has a fine school for engines. There are lessons in Whistle Blowing, Stopping for a Red Flag Waving, Puffing Loudly When Starting, Coming Around Curves Safely, Screeching When Stopping, and Clicking and Clacking Over the Rails.

Of all the things that are taught in the Lower Trainswitch School for Locomotives, the most important is, of course, Staying on the Rails No Matter What.

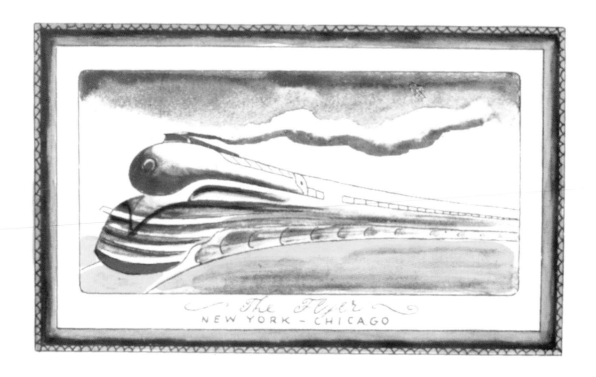

The Flyer
NEW YORK – CHICAGO

The head of the school is an old engineer named Bill. Bill always tells the new locomotives that he will not be angry if they sometimes spill the soup pulling the diner, or if they turn the milk to butter now and then. But they will never, never be good trains unless they get 100 A+ in Staying on the Rails No Matter What. All the baby engines work very hard to get 100 A+ in Staying on the Rails. After a few weeks not one of the engines in the Lower Trainswitch School for Locomotives would even think of getting off the rails, no matter—well, no matter what.

One day a new locomotive named Tootle came to school.

"Here is the finest baby I've seen since Old 600," thought Bill. He patted the gleaming young locomotive and said, "How would you like to grow up to be the Flyer between New York and Chicago?"

"If a Flyer goes very fast, I should like to be one," Tootle answered. "I love to go fast. Watch me."

He raced all around the roundhouse.
"Good! Good!" said Bill. "You must study
Whistle Blowing, Puffing Loudly When Starting,
Stopping for a Red Flag Waving, and Pulling the
Diner Without Spilling the Soup.

"But most of all, you must study Staying on the Rails No Matter What. Remember, you can't be a Flyer unless you get 100 A+ in Staying on the Rails."

Tootle promised that he would remember and that he would work very hard.

He did, too.

He even worked hard at Stopping for a Red Flag Waving. Tootle did not like those lessons at all. There is nothing a locomotive hates more than stopping.

But Bill said that no locomotive ever, ever kept going when he saw a red flag waving.

One day, while Tootle was practicing for his lesson in Staying on the Rails No Matter What, a dreadful thing happened.

He looked across the meadow he was running through and saw a fine, strong black horse.

"Race you to the river!" shouted the black horse and kicked up his heels.

Away went the horse. His black tail streamed out behind him and his mane tossed in the wind. Oh, how he could run!

"Here I go," said Tootle to himself.

"If I am going to be a Flyer, I can't let a horse beat me," he puffed. "Everyone at school will laugh at me."

His wheels turned so fast that they were silver streaks. The cars lurched and bumped together. And just as Tootle was sure he could win, the tracks made a great curve.

"Oh, Whistle!" cried Tootle. "That horse will beat me now. He'll run straight while I take the Great Curve."

Then the Dreadful Thing happened. After all that Bill had said about Staying on the Rails No Matter What, Tootle jumped off the tracks and raced alongside the black horse!

The race ended in a tie. Both Tootle and the black horse were happy. They stood on the bank of the river and talked.

"It's nice here in the meadow," Tootle said.

When Tootle got back to school, he said nothing about leaving the rails. But he thought about it that night in the roundhouse.

"Tomorrow I will work hard," decided Tootle.
"I will not even think of leaving the rails, no
matter what."

And he did work hard. He practiced tootling
so much that the Mayor Himself ran up the hill,
his green coattails flapping, and said that
everyone in the village had a headache and
would he please stop TOOTLING.

So Tootle was sent to practice Staying on the
Rails No Matter What.

As he came to the Great Curve, Tootle looked across the meadow. It was full of buttercups.

"It's like a big yellow carpet. How I should like to play in them and hold one under my searchlight to see if I like butter!" thought Tootle. "But no, I am going to be a Flyer and I must practice Staying on the Rails No Matter What!"

Tootle clicked and clacked around the Great Curve. His wheels began to say over and over again, "Do you like butter? Do you?"

"I don't know," said Tootle crossly. "But I'm going to find out."

He stopped much faster than any good Flyer ever does, unless he is Stopping for a Red Flag Waving. He hopped off the tracks and bumped along the meadow to the yellow buttercups.

"What fun!" said Tootle.

And he danced around and around and held one of the buttercups under his searchlight.

"I do like butter!" cried Tootle. "I do!"

At last the sun began to go down, and it was time to hurry to the roundhouse.

That evening while the Chief Oiler was playing checkers with old Bill, he said, "It's queer. It's very queer, but I found grass between Tootle's front wheels today."

"Hmm," said Bill. "There must be grass growing on the tracks."

"Not on our tracks," said the Day Watchman, who spent his days watching the tracks and his nights watching Bill and the Chief Oiler play checkers.

Bill's face was stern. "Tootle knows he must get 100 A+ in Staying on the Rails No Matter What if he is going to be a Flyer."

Next day Tootle played all day in the meadow. He watched a green frog and he made a daisy chain. He found a rain barrel, and he said softly, "Toot!" "TOOT!" shouted the barrel. "Why, I sound like a Flyer already!" cried Tootle.

That night the First Assistant Oiler said he had found a daisy in Tootle's bell. The day after that, the Second Assistant Oiler said that he had found hollyhock flowers floating in Tootle's eight bowls of soup.

And then the Mayor Himself said that he had seen Tootle chasing butterflies in the meadow. The Mayor Himself said that Tootle had looked very silly, too.

Early one morning Bill had a long, long talk with the Mayor Himself.

When the Mayor Himself left the Lower Trainswitch School for Locomotives, he laughed all the way to the village.

"Bill's plan will surely put Tootle back on the track," he chuckled.

Bill ran from one store to the next, buying ten yards of this and twenty yards of that and all you have of the other. The Chief Oiler and the First, Second, and Third Assistant Oilers were hammering and sawing instead of oiling and polishing. And Tootle? Well, Tootle was in the meadow watching the butterflies flying and wishing he could dip and soar as they did.

Not a store in Lower Trainswitch was open the next day and not a person was at home. By the time the sun came up, every villager was hiding in the meadow along the tracks. And each of them had a red flag. It had taken all the red goods in Lower Trainswitch, and hard work by the Oilers, but there was a red flag for everyone.

Soon Tootle came tootling happily down the
tracks. When he came to the meadow, he hopped
off the tracks and rolled along the grass. Just as
he was thinking what a beautiful day it was, a
red flag poked up from the grass and waved
hard. Tootle stopped, for every locomotive knows
he must Stop for a Red Flag Waving.

"I'll go another way," said Tootle.

He turned to the left, and up came another waving red flag, this time from the middle of the buttercups.

When he went to the right, there was another red flag waving.

There were red flags waving from the buttercups, in the daisies, under the trees, near the bluebirds' nest, and even one behind the rain barrel. And, of course, Tootle had to stop for each one, for a locomotive must always Stop for a Red Flag Waving.

"Red flags," muttered Tootle. "This meadow is full of red flags. How can I have any fun?

"Whenever I start, I have to stop. Why did I think this meadow was such a fine place? Why don't I ever see a green flag?"

Just as the tears were ready to slide out of his boiler, Tootle happened to look back over his coal car. On the tracks stood Bill, and in his hand was a big green flag. "Oh!" said Tootle.

He puffed up to Bill and stopped.

"This is the place for me," said Tootle. "There is nothing but red flags for locomotives that get off their tracks."

"Hurray!" shouted the people of Lower Trainswitch, and they jumped up from their hiding places. "Hurray for Tootle the Flyer!"

Now Tootle is a famous Two-Miles-a-Minute Flyer. The young locomotives listen to his advice. "Work hard," he tells them. "Always remember to Stop for a Red Flag Waving. But most of all, Stay on the Rails No Matter What."

THE HAPPY MAN
AND HIS
DUMP TRUCK

By Miryam

Once upon a time there was a man who had a dump truck.

Every time he saw a friend, he would wave his hand and tip the dumper.

One day he was riding in his dump truck, singing a happy song, when he met a pig going along the road.

"Would you like a ride in my dump truck?"
he asked.

"Oh, thank you!" said the pig. And he
climbed into the back of the truck.

After they had gone a little way down the
road, the man saw a friend.

He waved his hand and tipped the dumper.

"Whee," said the pig. "What fun!" And he slid all the way down to the bottom of the dumper.

Very soon they came to a farm.

"Here is where my friends live," said the
pig. "You have a nice dump truck.

"Would you please let my friends see your truck?"

"I will give them a ride in my dump truck," said the man.

So the hen and the rooster climbed into the
truck.

And the duck climbed into the truck.

And the dog and the cat climbed into the truck.

And the pig climbed back into the truck, too.

And the man closed the tailgate, so they would not fall out.

And then off they went!
They went past the farm, and all the
animals waved to the farmer.

The man was very happy. "They are all my friends," he said.

So he waved his hand and tipped the dumper.

The hen, the rooster, the duck, the dog, the cat, and the pig all slid down the dumper into a big heap!

The animals were all so happy!
Then the man took them for a long ride,
and drove them back to the farm.

He opened the tailgate wide and raised the dumper all the way up.

All the animals slid off the truck onto the ground.

"What a fine sliding board," they all said.

"Thank you," said all the animals.

"Cut, cut," clucked the hen.

"Cock-a-doodle-doo," the rooster crowed.

"Quack, quack,"
quacked the duck.

"Bow-wow,"
barked the dog.
"Meow, meow,"
mewed the cat.

And the pig said a great big grunt. "Oink, oink!"

The man waved his hand and tipped the dumper, and he rode off in his dump truck, singing a happy song.

SCUFFY
THE TUGBOAT

And His Adventures Down The River

By Gertrude Crampton

Scuffy was sad.

Scuffy was cross.

Scuffy sniffed his blue smokestack.

"A toy store is no place for a red-painted tugboat," said Scuffy, and he sniffed his blue smokestack again. "I was meant for bigger things."

"Perhaps you would not be cross if you went sailing," said the man with the polka-dot tie, who owned the shop.

So one night he took Scuffy home to his little boy. He filled the bathtub with water.

"Sail, little tugboat," said the little boy.

"I won't sail in a bathtub," said Scuffy. "A tub is no place for a red-painted tugboat. I was meant for bigger things."

The next day the man with the polka-dot tie and his little boy carried Scuffy to a laughing brook that started high in the hills.

"Sail, little tugboat," said the man with the polka-dot tie.

It was Spring, and the brook was full to the brim with its water. And the water moved in a hurry, as all things move in a hurry when it is Spring.

Scuffy was in a hurry, too.

"Come back, little tugboat, come back,"
cried the little boy as the hurrying, brimful
brook carried Scuffy downstream.

"Not I," tooted Scuffy. "Not I. This is the life
for me."

All that day Scuffy sailed along with the brook.

Past the meadows filled with cowslips. Past the women washing clothes on the bank. Past the little woods filled with violets.

Cows came to the brook to drink.

They stood in the cool water, and it was fun

to sail around between their legs and bump
softly into their noses.

It was fun to see them drink.

But when a white-and-brown cow almost
drank Scuffy instead of the brook's cool water,
Scuffy was frightened. That was not fun!

Night came, and with it the moon.

There was nothing to see but the quiet trees.

Suddenly an owl called out, "Hoot! Hooot!"

"Toot, tooot!" cried the frightened tugboat, and he wished he could see the smiling face of the man with the polka-dot tie.

When morning came, Scuffy was cross instead of frightened.

"I was meant for bigger things, but which way am I to go?" he said. But there was only one way to go, and that was with the running water where the two brooks met to form a small river. And with the river sailed Scuffy, the red-painted tugboat.

He was proud when he sailed past villages.
"People build villages at the edge of my
river," said Scuffy, and he straightened his
blue smokestack.

Once Scuffy's river joined a small one jammed with logs. Here were men in heavy jackets and great boots, walking about on the floating logs, trying to pry them free.

"Toot, toot, let me through," demanded Scuffy. But the men paid no attention to him. They pushed the logs apart so they would drift with the river to the sawmill in the town. Scuffy bumped along with the jostling logs.

"Ouch!" he cried as two logs bumped together.

"This is a fine river," said Scuffy, "but it's very busy and very big for me."

He was proud when he sailed under the bridges.

"My river is so wide and so deep that people must build bridges to cross it."

The river moved through big towns now instead of villages.

And the bridges over it were very wide—
wide enough so that many cars and trucks
and streetcars could cross all at once.

The river got deeper and deeper. Scuffy did
not have to tuck up his bottom.

The river moved faster and faster.

"I feel like a train instead of a tugboat,"
said Scuffy as he was hurried along.

He was proud when he passed the old
sawmill with its waterwheel.

But high in the hills and mountains the winter snow melted. Water filled the brooks and rushed from there into the small rivers. Faster and faster it flowed, to the great river where Scuffy sailed.

"There is too much water in this river," said Scuffy as he pitched and tossed on the waves. "Soon it will splash over the top and what a flood there will be!"

Soon great armies of men came to save the fields and towns from the rushing water.

They filled bags with sand and put them at the edge of the river.

"They're making higher banks for the river," shouted Scuffy, "to hold the water back." The water rose higher and higher.

The men built the sandbags higher and higher. Higher! went the river. Higher! went the sandbags.

At last the water rose no more. The floodwater rushed on to the sea, and Scuffy raced along with the flood. The people and the fields and the towns were safe.

On went the river to the sea. At last Scuffy
sailed into a big city. Here the river widened,
and all about were docks and wharves.

Oh, it was a busy place and a noisy place! The cranes groaned as they swung the cargoes into great ships. The porters shouted as they carried suitcases and boxes on board.

Horses stamped and truck motors roared, streetcars clanged and people shouted. Scuffy said, "Toot, toot," but nobody noticed.

"Oh, oh!" cried Scuffy when he saw the sea. "There is no beginning and there is no end to the sea. I wish I could find the man with the polka-dot tie and his little boy!"

Just as the little red-painted tugboat sailed past the last piece of land, a hand reached out and picked him up. And there was the man with the polka-dot tie, with his little boy beside him.

Scuffy is home now with the man with the polka-dot tie and his little boy.

He sails from one end of the bathtub to the other.

"This is the place for a red-painted tugboat," says Scuffy. "And this is the life for me."

About Tibor Gergely

❧

When he arrived in New York City from Europe on the eve of World War II, Tibor Gergely had with him nothing more than a suitcase or two, a dozen rolled-up canvases, and a handful of drawings. By the time of Gergely's death in 1978, the work of this Hungarian-born artist was known and loved by millions of children, both in America and around the world.

It was the Artists and Writers Guild in New York that first recognized a potential children's book illustrator in Gergely. The mischievous sense of humor in his drawings, along with the bold outlines and bright colors, was sure to appeal to children. When the Little Golden Book series was created by the Artists and Writers Guild in the early 1940s, Gergely soon established himself as a favorite illustrator. His work is still held in the highest regard.

A self-taught artist, Gergely remembered being inspired to draw for the first time at the age of four when he saw a set of medieval woodcuts. Much later, the vivid paintings of the Flemish master Breughel influenced him deeply. At the age of twenty, he went to Vienna and began his career as a newspaper cartoonist. He was also a successful stage designer and cofounded a marionette theater. Gergely was a serious painter, too, and returned to Budapest in 1931 to help found the Atelier Art School and to continue his painting.

As a children's book illustrator, Tibor Gergely brought to life two of the most famous of all the Little Golden Book characters, Tootle the train and Scuffy the toy tugboat, each represented in this collection. Tootle and Scuffy have both been described as creatures with a taste for mischief and adventure. Strangely enough, friends described Tibor Gergely in the very same way, expanding the artist's portrait to say he was also especially gentle, sensitive, and humane.

In 1954, Gergely illustrated a book published by Lippincott titled *The Wheel on the Chimney*. That work won him the much-prized Caldecott Honor Award.